Fading Lullabies

A Collection of Gothic Poems

By Dale M. Chatwin

ISBN: 9781701654679

Printed in the United Kingdom

Cover Design by Nikki Rennie-Smith © 2019

dalemchatwin@icloud.com

Dedicated To You

Underneath the Draconian Sky

My emotions have been swathed,
The pencil lead has been engaged.
It's appealing to the spirit mind on several levels.
I've looked for that matchstick once maybe
several.

To be found under a curtain, swaying softly
Silently in time with a beat
And discover a reptilian mentality is our only feat.
A song plays heavily like thunder
Breaking west on the horizon.
Can you smell the salt drifting easterly
From the monochrome mountains?
Travelling on dust on particles
That breach a certain rule
A certain test for a fallen mule.

Being here amongst cacti I burn and swim

In a melodic, almost fashionable heat.

Mincing through rock and minuscule insects

I try not to sting, to step, to destroy.

The sun is beating now

I can hear its dull drum tap, tap, tap

Forever producing more bass,

Less snare, more crash, less ride,

With the occasional clang of a bell.

My head aches.

Body wet, dripping oh so wet, and sticky

From the salty sweat I can taste on my lips,

With cracked skin they bleed.

I need rest,

I need feed,

I need water forever.

I need transport home.

With the endless miles and endless walking
One feels like one is trapped under a dome of
Impenetrable transparent steel.
Metallic after taste breeds only like a virus
If one lets one's mind become vulnerable
In these harsh climates.

Where down the line did my life come to this?
Did it boil down to the factual events
Of my complacent, habitual style of living?
Or did I just happen to let fate seep its tendrils
Softly, spasmodically under my crotch?
Either way I am here.
No escape.
Just keep treading to take the bait.

Same old strip, same old road,
Different boxes
And sexual modes of desire.
I must be delirious.

How long have I been without water?
Keep track, keep time...
How can one keep track of time
In a space so destitute,
So devoid of procreation?

I know not the answer;
I don't even wear a watch,
Just a compass on my wrist,
And with the right kind of vision
It could almost be a chronographer.

But alas, that stage has not been set in the part
Where your brain has thirst for moisture
And shrivels like an elderly penis.
No trace of hallucinogen in
This forest of secrets.

The stars are out tonight,
Sheep bray in the distance.

I lie in a ditch with dust for a blanket

And in my mind a guitar licks a solo.

Cold and hollow.

Sleep is not an issue here

For the question of whether my eyes will close

Is still at a crossroads.

I saw a landscape that could cook the very fabric

Of Satan's hoof prints.

When this dark settles

It could freeze the world

Into a delirious ice age.

The body shivers and

The mind rots in a sense of self deliverance.

Then one by one my digits fall apart.

It starts with the toes, big first, getting smaller.

There is no pain in this unforgiving act.

Just a robotic emotion to toy with,

I begin piece together a solemn jigsaw
of random thought.

"Why is this happening?"
I whispered,
Although there was no need to.
This habit turns on automatically
In these late hours.

There was something almost epically apocalyptic
In watching my vessel decompose,
In the cold dry evening under Orion's belt,
The strangest sensation that one has ever felt.

To be left alone in this strange dimension,
Questioning the how's and whys,
To experience such obscurity
Without the essence of being high,
To watch one's slow and gradual demise;
Underneath a draconian sky.

Quixotic Revelations

The cold chills my bones

Like hypodermic needles scratching stone,

I rose from the gutter,

Thoughts fractured and cluttered,

Made my way back home,

Uninterrupted, the streets were deserted,

The wind howled,

The sound was a choir of souls,

Lamenting their former selves,

Anguished they roam,

Through purgatory, their home.

Now it is done,

The humming has ceased,

I asked the wind: "why?"

The answer whistled through trees,

Across the ocean, in my dreams.

"It is your time,"

I heard it say.

A circle formed,

I fell into ancient territory,

Followed the rocks, erect and docile,

Along a misty peak,

Fighting the wind, failing, dissolving.

An entity lingered

In that hyperborean breeze,

Transforming me, full of deceit,

Tendrils touched licking my cheeks,

Blood rushed, becoming crimson,

Tears tried to exude, failing, dissolving.

The rocks fuelled this insanity,

Driving me to the realisation,

It is all an embodiment of me,

Every piece of gravel

A symbol of my mistrust,

A legacy demolished,

An application of my shame.

The skirmish betwixt the elements and myself
Concluded with a hunt where I was the prey,
If I was caught, my sins would be weighed,
Tossed from the mountain if I did not obey.

I was being taunted
By quixotic revelations,
Building tensions,
For the rest of my days,
All I wanted was to lay
In bed, sleeping away
The delusions, the ghouls,
The stalking elements,
I feel like a fool.

I could not fathom the world I occupied,
What happened on those frigid streets?
A circle had formed, yet I did not retreat,

Instead I tumbled to the rhythm of my heartbeat,

Quickening its pace I tried, and tried,

To prevent the descent, now I cry and cry.

I cannot hide from the elements,

Those embodiments of despair,

My soul laid out bare,

I am the heir to my ancestors' sins,

My skin blood red, a vestige of a nightmare,

Trapped behind my children's eyes,

A by-product of their distraught minds.

First published in Star & Crescent magazine on 27th January 2017.

Earthly Insanity

I'd rather be here
Where sanity mutates
Into glorious murals of madness,
I'd rather talk to my saviour,
A subterranean dweller
Playing with my veins
Like strings, a puppeteer.

I'd rather run here
Where my fears evolve
Into shining stars,
Where supermen find new careers
And die alone in solitary towns.

I'd rather be in love
Where we can roam hand in hand,
Face to face with fate,

Not knowing where we are,
Two zeroes lost in space,
And I can wipe tears of lust
From your make up smeared face.
I'd rather crawl inside my mind
Where the heart cannot find
Me cowering in fear,
A filthy lesson in voyeurism,
A lonely guy in reality,
No company can sate my appetite
For a doomsday sonnet.

I'd rather be pleasured
Where shadows can witness
The sins of my soul,
Chasing diseases up steep stairs,
Their worth is cheaply haggled,
Rotting in a sour day
Touching my needful body.

I'd rather be in an urn
Where people can touch my remains,
My ashes seeping through hands,
An orgy of mourning,
An ugly rumour unhappily spread
Through synthetic emotions,
Until their duplicitous work is done.

I'd rather be dirty
So the devil can haunt me,
An isolated boy with no control,
Shaping my life with dreams,
Memories of oddities,
Dancing with you,
My earthly insanity.

Forever Falling

Butchered filth I left you to drown
In the sanguine seas of decay,
While I,
Sleepless, livid,
Played with your dreams of fate
That began to fray at my touch.

I sank into the quagmire of contempt,
Reminiscing about all the savage days I spent,
Digging a trench in the soft peaty bog,
My callous hands being ready to flog
My organic rag doll as we prepare to feed.

A Speckled Dwarf succoured
Me with an arduous task,
Its tusks were awe inspiring ivory,

Its hair was coarse
And it wailed like a Banshee.
It spluttered and hacked out other worlds.
Infinite worlds shrouded in crystal bubbles.

There was a pallid orchid
Staring through a dungeon window,
Peering at the blots of morning dew,
Wondering how its journey had ended there,
One that began high in the mountains
Soaring above the monochrome desert,
Immersed in foggy solitude,
Regretting the sorrow and fear.

A cacophonous metallic screech
Pierced the drums of my inner ear,
Followed by the bass roar
Of an unpleasant Daemon,
My eyes beheld a yawning cavern
Wherein my destiny lay.

Tears, viscous,

A residue released from my

Treacherous emotional feature,

Down my solemn cheek,

Embedded in the ancient hourglass

That embraces my soul,

My sweat reeks of death.

Frenzied froth bubbled

And broiled from my mouth,

Madness took my brain so soft,

Playing with it like putty,

This is my fate,

My doom takes a dive

Into the pit of tormented hate.

Forever falling.

Save me from this cacophonous hive.

Silence.

On the horrific hallows I lay trembling,

The alluvium beneath my broken cadaver

Expelled toxic fumes.

I had no choice but to breathe.

Glutinous tentacles writhed

And felt their way over my corpse

Slowly digesting me,

I wretched and heaved.

There was no sign

Of that perfidious Dwarf,

Confounded sprite whore.

So in these catacombs

I succumb to Death's tendrils.

Dying all alone and shunned by the angels.

Solitude

I am the watcher,

The abominable prisoner,

Solitude invited me here.

I fought battles, raised castles,

Set ablaze entire worlds,

Now solitude holds me near.

I froze hearts and brought tears

To those who found love,

Solitude fuelled their fear.

I've been the ensnared

The slave to passion,

Solitude punctured me like a spear.

I was the strong

But am now the weary emotional wreck,

Solitude is a friend so dear.

I lament for you who I lost in the spring,

When solitude settled in midyear.

It was a quiver, a bow; an arrow to my throat,

Solitude's poison is fatally severe.

Now I sit and lie in wait for my inexorable fate,

I have crossed the splintered bridges

And gouged the wood from my feet,

Waded in the freezing rivers

Where the water and ice meet,

The cold voice that greeted me

Was of a bitter descent,

I realised the words you spewed

Were never fully meant.

I was your knight,

Your dragon slayer as bold as brass,

Solitude launched me into a new frontier.

I am the gatekeeper, your resentful shadow,

Oh solitude you are always so sincere.

Past Hallucinations

Six-thirty in the morning
Feeling sticky on the floorboards,
With crust in my eyes,
Wiping away the disguise
From the night before.
Nostalgia was buoyant
In the lakes of my memories,
Creating God like effigies
From friends who played truant
Under the canopy
Of Dawn's winter brilliance,
Yawning like banshees
Ready to transcribe their diligence,
Redeeming features of
Numerological significance
Brought out my soul
Whispering fables with no control.

The boreal breeze chewed

My face and swallowed with contempt,

Today I will allude

To the girl whose death had commenced

At the hands of a bus driver,

Her bloodied body in the street,

That evening her parents couldn't find her,

Her untimely demise had been their defeat.

This day brought me gifts

Wrapped in polished barbed wire,

Recollections like haunting snowdrifts

Creating a remix of nature's choir,

Too early to pound a stake through the heart

Of vampiric beasts,

They lurk in the dark subconscious,

Too early to run endless miles

Around the Islands that left me beguiled.

So, where does it leave me, wizard of words?

Wave your magic wand to construe

The bastards who left me submerged

Within your curse, oh wizard of words,

Give me a synonym for every emotion

Caused by the pain of past hallucinations,

When I read transcriptions

Written by friends during mental revelations,

Brought on by intoxicants triggering

Imagination, a desperation of my subconscious,

Secrets of lives that came before us,

Revealed in dreams with eyes opened wide.

If I close my eyes,

Then reopen,

Will the colours evolve?

Will the textures of

Gravel transform?

Will the quality change

In the murky ocean

When I drift into sleep

With a passionate question?

It's only an estimation

Brought on by my superstition

Of those past hallucinations.

A Soft Haiku

The sea silt kicked up a saccharine stench,

From the untimely fathoms of its infested bed,

Weird Barnacle Beasts busied themselves,

Scuttling in moon like movements,

In their Arthropod magnificence

They fed off the emotions

Of Aquatic Amphibians,

Leaving their souls stagnant.

My posture was set on the shores of time,

Fixed gaze like a salient statue,

Cataclysmically I swam in a torrent

Of fertile betrayal,

As the froth of waves lapped tenderly

I wrote for you a soft Haiku:

I see a red star

Slow burn on the horizon
I wait with you there

In those leaden clouds I saw an imprint of you,
As our star set serenely on its shimmering horizon
I cast my thoughts to those days
Where we shared a simple solitude,
We fired electric silk across our naked taboos,
My fingers tracking across your heart,
Entangled in an intense embrace.

Now I am free,
Where land and ocean clasp hands,
The sensation of the cool zephyr
Is like your touch on this volcanic coastline,
The flow of air makes my face blush crimson,
My skin flakes and like ashes
I am slowly breathed back into the ocean,
Whispering a soft Haiku:

For you I decline
While chaos laments for us
And our star burns true

Winner of Editor's Poem of the Day on The
Poetry Forum: 30th July 2011

Dungeon of Doom

I'm in this dungeon of doom
Where these shackles protrude from my flesh
As the elements exude through the bars
And the days mesh into months,
Until I received the news of you, my dear,
Away so far so only the heart can desire.

My memory is a falsity
Of you, of us, of everything we used to be,
Through this humble hole in the wall
I can smell the briny air,
I long to drift with you
Upon the salty seas to see how we fare
In the wide world.

Unburdened by guilt, our regrets will unfurl
Of a murder we once shared,

Gruesome, grisly, a synonym

For every sinew I saw you tear

From his wretched body,

A cadaver made unholy by your hands.

Afterwards we rolled together in the sands,

Naked, in blood and matrimony,

A fleeting fancy, the next day you abandoned me,

I was caught, I could have fought,

But my thoughts were hazy,

An aftershock of your treachery.

Now in this letter I hear you are coming,

To watch me swinging with my neck in a noose,

I wonder if you'll loosen the knot,

I doubt it.

In this dungeon of doom

These shackles protrude, making me ache,

The image of your face in the crowd

Throws a shroud over my plight,

A desperate fight when my legs begin to thrash

And I begin to die.

I will look into your eyes,

You will be surprised

By the love I still harbour for you,

One day the truth will catch up with you too.

The Ultimate Passage

The sapphire heavens opened a doorway
Above the streaked clouds,
Staring in wonderment at its glassy texture,
The moist calefaction within my soul
Leaving me submitted and aroused.

Taking seven steps along
The tire beaten concrete,
I yield to this super incumbent force,
Fixed between the land and the stars,
Now I glide in measurement across
The everlasting void of continuous imprints
Left behind be senile immortals,
We are children of the dead beat.

I pursued in trance a flock of bemused faces,
Expressions of a lost cause,

Set in congregation of cheap
Lethargic flaws.

A glitch flashed, then a talisman passed
Through the fathoms of time,
A key of granite to be infused with
The threshold, waiting beyond,
Within a gospel for us,
A means to renounce responsibility
And abscond.

Simplicity our minds can't handle,
Instead we chose to rabble and ramble
Through the paths that brought
Us exquisite struggle,
I know deep down our salvation
Lies in the gems aloft,
Those slices of void,
Cut with inexplicable razors,
Waiting for me to show her

Where I stand, and reprimand the heavens,

For allowing me to wander for the first time

Through the ultimate passage I cannot define,

But I cannot lie, I love how it ends,

Launching into the stars

With a cosmological bends.

Exhaustion

There's a blister on my ankle,
It broke today
From the miles I walked,
A small patch of blood on the white sock,
I should be home asleep in my dock.

Exhaustion is my best friend
In this early hour,
My mind is a mess
I guess this is a test,
Muscles ache and feet sting,
I'll see what the day brings.

Sleep.
Should I sleep on concrete paved sheets?
I'm too tired to make the journey back.

Exhaustion is my ally my true natured alibi,

The rants of a tired man

Forever knotting the noose.

There are amber lights,

Cracks in my reality,

Come here, share this feeling,

Walk alongside me.

Two red lights in the sky

From a tower so white and high,

I could touch it in a dream,

If I only I were at home.

Alone.

Dreaming.

Instead I walk half an hour,

Always losing power,

Being in a state of mindless thought

At this road of squares,

Fraught with tired spit stains,
And chewing gum glue.

Bus stop lights, car lamps and street signs
Illuminate in my eyes,
My pupils dilate creeping
Into my spine.
It is time.
Destination reached.

Fill in the gaps of my arduous journey,
Where time goes fast and illusion seems to last,
I arrived home in a heap
Of clothes and toothpaste,
I stripped and dropped on the bed with haste,
The lamp switched off, my mind went blank,
I thank myself and shut my mind,
My eyes closed like lead.
I'm dead to the world now I'm at peace,
And my body can regain the energy it has drained,

I'll sleep now, I'll wait till morning's light,
And not wake up without a fight.

Primitive Times Primitive Highs

A cold hand grasps at my feet,
It pulls me slowly into the damp sheets,
A universe I will find, twisting blackening
Tunnel vision blind,
An echo blasts within my thoughts warning me
Of this onslaught.

The cold hand that pulled,
The damp hand that grabbed,
Its fingers and nails softly clad with the velvet
Of a deity long forgot,
Fed from the bubbling fleshpot,
My grey and weary mascot.

They will chase me down the hole
These questioning thoughts of mine,
Into the recesses of my soul,

These times and highs are divine,
It's not something that evolved
Out of my Primitive Fashion,
Neither a situation softly resolved,
To absolve me of my passion.

We are smashing stones of granite
To remind us that it's real,
A world of dogma puppet shows,
I'll coagulate the steel,
Build me a tower, a legendary structure
As part of the story,
Repetitive repetition over and over,
Eventually they will agree.

Suddenly I came to see,
This world that has been affecting me,
I've climbed twisted mountains,
Observed the shifting poles,
Witnessed the faces of these vile trolls,

The ones that eat out precious dreams.

Of all my dysfunctional delusions
I've sniggered at these rabid persecutions,
I've indulged once too often
In the truffles of the heathens,
Begged for logic, begged for reason,
Begged for a solution
To this degenerate pollution,
All I find amidst the commotion
Is an ocean of fear
Drawing me near into the embrace
Of primitive thought
And an endless rat race.

Severn Valley Beat

White summer flakes
Drifting delicately on a lucid current,
The Pagan God's luminosity beams
(*Everything serves the beam*)
Unbroken on the landscape,
Witnessing its sullen gold flakes.

Industrial steam bellows
From a wide girth,
My smoking is prohibited,
Churning coal diminishing,
Incandescent fire flourishing,
Burning, searing,
The aroma of cauterized air
Clogs my facial centrepiece.

Faces of stupefaction lean,

Savage reactions from the side lines
Mean the timetable was wrong,
A ghost from the '40s fleeing the scene.

There are blotches on the wood paint,
Signs from an era woefully built,
The quality of turf leaves passengers
With an inspired sense of guilt.
"Get to grips with the Midlands" I read,
"Breed more pigs use Thorley's Feed!"
These words, the rust,
The discombobulated clutter,
Viewing the skies
As the springtime birds flutter.

Disconcerted voices babble,
Butchering the silence,
While thick ash is bestowed from above,
In a charcoal deluge,
Chug, chug, chug,

It hollers, howls,

Screeches within its time bubble,

Perceptions of its glory being ever so humble.

"Players please give up your fee,

The price is steep to ensure your glee!"

An excited voice booms into my ears,

What, there's a carnival?

Candy floss aromas and jingle jangle bells,

Bustling children filling the atmosphere

With unsatisfied yells.

The journey isn't over,

Never at the end,

Never admit defeat,

Clunking, clunking,

Observing the earth photosynthesise

Into the endless chasm,

That chasm, that canyon,

I tripped, heard a snap,

Jolted awake

I must have momentarily

Sent my consciousness

Into a warped slice of existence,

But oh, I'm still here,

Trapped in the bliss of the steam engine hiss.

A Captured Moment

I procrastinate on a deserted seat,

Feeling the waves lap at my feet,

I look above at a greying sky,

Yesterday was so beautiful,

The pebbled beach seems immovable,

White froth bubbles and squeaks

On rolls of water,

The waves move one for the other,

I watch from my place on shingles and grain,

Crane my head down to my feet

Bare and dirty.

A dismal scenario that may depress,

It may stir a degrading emotion,

But I see a beauty in that unforgiving ocean

Because my heart is strong and full of life,

I'll sit here and watch and ponder and wonder,

Where do I go from here?

Bar Fly

Scattered claps in a dark club,

Can you hear the sound against the black walls?

There are sketches of bands from yesteryears,

A place that once thrived off the fears

Of many a leather clad being,

A band plays out a petty performance on a stage

Of strobing coloured lights,

I watch through my bar fly eyes

Pool tables and expressions,

A small crowd paying attention,

It's just another showcase of the amateur sessions.

I'll sit and drink myself into a stupor,

As an unknown shadow,

Thinking of friends long gone,

Allowing nostalgia to wash me clean,

The music tears through the ears of clientele,

They came to hear someone else.

Just rock and sway,
Just think of yourself,
Feel the chairs of wood
How they ruin your posture,
Feel the vibes of bass and drum,
This is a night to shun the ones
Who came to see another.

I feel this verse is on a tangent,
I feel your eyes,
Your mind grows weary of my ramblings.

The night is not too bad,
I feel I've had a chance to speak my mind,
Taking life off rewind,
When the instruments stop,
I'll walk and talk
With a friend from long ago,

About an age that was beautiful,

A place in my thoughts imprinted on this world.

Return

It is I who should fly in the seas of desire,

To lay many roads and douse many fires,

I'll form the stone brick by brick

It will be there forever until it sticks.

It's me, the man who waits for her

To return from her wanderings

Amongst the fir,

I'll cool in the ice to return to her.

She was the girl

Whose beauty stayed my hand,

We wandered for years upon days,

In salty seas, upon tender sands,

She wanted more till time was done,

Stripping me of my soul until I was gone.

She'll follow aimlessly and lead blind

In lands of shallow climes,

So I'll wait in this endless ocean

Counting the fish that float on by,

They'll watch me and look,

I'll pay no heed,

My mind has been set

On who I need.

This is the first poem I ever wrote in 2010 at twenty-two years old.

I Found the End of Summer
on Dorset's Sapphire Shores

Uranium welded to your smile
Radiating a sickly pulse of jealousy,
Lapsing phosphorescence
From the piercing eyes of a child,
Achieving the molten effect
Of diminishing purity.

Return from the centre of a
Bullet laden storm,
You of all folk,
Young in mind,
Aged in organs,
Shedding the scales from
Your procrastinating form.

The exaltation steaming from your pores,

Bred with excited sneers,

Dimensions aplenty through solid oak doors,

Hermes; slayer of giants, expels a gust,

Uprooting mountains,

While flowers of sweet peach flesh

Radiate the last of Gaia's spores.

This was the end of summer

On Dorset's sapphire shores.

This grotto I inhabit releases

A sickly incense of excrement braised

By a commode chef,

Writhing into my nostrils.

"I phoned my daughter she's alright,

Went to visit her Dad's grave,"

I heard beside me in the damp tingle

Of summer's final breath.

"My Nan was 57 when she died,"

Another voice spoke,

Conversations so bleak this night

As the moon smirks from above,

Its gentle indifference

Settling in my hair.

Skipping through poppies,

Maroon opium chants,

Fattening bees,

From their buzzing blinding rants,

Memories wash into shore,

Like a tsunami in the mind,

Fossils in ancient rock,

I could not possibly find.

Winner of Editor's Poem of the Day and Editor's Poem of the Week on The Poetry Forum: 23rd and 29h August 2011

A Lover's Paranoia

They kissed beneath
The iron clad vault above,
Soaking in the refreshing drink
Of summer rain,
Their hair, silk woven,
Entwined by a breeze,
Forfeiting their perils
Of bitter loss.

A Seagull, bloated,
A gluttonous specimen of the cliffs,
Swooped down and scooped up
Vomit spattered on the pavement,
The organic residue of the night before
When they shared their
Midriff pact.

Speech,

His only form of true expression,

Cast out!

Replaced by raving lunacy,

Stumbling on a revelation

(Amidst the sour taste of

Stagnant bile and yeast

Through the winding path of

Broken memories,

Splintered glass slicing

His tongue),

That her actions have fallen upon

Many a bodice,

Knowing no truth.

Quaking over his oral action,

There was a network

Of rusty gravestones

Laden with the diamond embers

Of fresh fallen snow,

Each with its own sun,
Burning incandescently,
He had put his heart into the hands
Of someone who lacked the concept
Of love.

On the far borders
The land itself produced its own stars,
Winking amber and distant red dwarfs.

"I felt the wheel of a lullaby turn
Slowly within my skin,
There's a lesser truth set to swallow me
With bloodied knives,
When the night speaks
Of silence in the halls,
I'll rap my piano for you to sleep,
Weary maid, charm of my dreams."

He spoke, a trinket of her opal obsession,
While his gaze switched in wonderment
From her eyes to the horizon.

"I'll meet you there,
Inside the chest of imagination,
I hid my insinuations within my sleep
Marked with thudding burden
Of last nights concentrated crowds
Sinking into their crying intent.
Feeling my strength being all but spent."

She spoke and caressed his hands,
A caress pulsing in pimples of flesh.

Splashes of tangerine,
Scorched the deep blue
Of another evening,
With the rebirth of the solar ring
Come pioneers of amethyst crystals

Scattered neatly across
A blanket of emerald.

Dusting off their clothes,
The estranged couple part ways,
Using nature's springs to wash away
The previous hours.

When they slept,
Each dreamt of a piano
Of polished mahogany
Being played by their heart's token,
Rhythmic fluency being spoken.

The Delivery Room

In this lounge we wait

In heat and melting into

The ooze of employment training:

"Fill in these forms,

Tick all these boxes,

We want to help you,

We promise,"

But it's all lies,

To move you on,

What can I say in here?

Do I have to adhere

To the dogmatic scripture

Of the looming Job Centre?

Creeping shadows fall

Onto my brow,

A bald man, Bob, left ear pierced

(He looked like my father)
In a maroon shirt
Led us to our doom,
Paperwork,
So many dead trees
To please officials,
Induction tribunals
Shoved in my face,
A sense of duty.

In the delivery room we're lined up,
Like whores in Amsterdam,
To be taken by the soulless
Who want to scam,
What's behind?
The way always finds you
Gradually you're here forever.

Kaleidoscopic caverns,
Psychedelic patterns,

What did he say?

I switched off,

The imps were back

In the woodwork

When I lost it,

Wailing,

Aromas of coconut

Of Old Spice,

Wafting,

Throwing my weight

Around the delivery room,

While three looked upon me

With horrific admiration,

As I plunged my pen

Into Bob's throat.

He was still talking,

(He looks like my father!)

I was perspiring,

My mental travels

Cost me my patience,

A delay in time,

An illusion ruptured.

A selfish road

In the low territories,

I fled from this China house

Of porcelain dolls

And stained white walls.

Winner of Editor's Poem of the Day on The Poetry Forum: 3rd November 2011

Standing Outside Smoking

An e-bow droned hypnotically in my ear,
The stars are pimples of light
Penetrating the black
Silk veil of night's embrace,
A seductive voice pulled
Me into serenity.

Amber beams reflecting on
Oceans of concrete in quiet streets,
Dents of rock catching pockets
Of light in my glazed vision.

Is this reality feasible in my perception?
Are my thoughts a trailing mist?
Floating in waves,
Above my cranium,
Clouds of aluminium,

Ripped blotches of dull delight.

Take flight with me-

Aviation-

Take my hand-

Infinity create-

Be my soul spun on a web

Of loving cotton-

These memories we share-

Never forgotten-

Journey to Another Ocean

Another doom laden day slips away
And the land is dark and cold,
I see my world through a small glass window
Where weeds strive to grow,
Another night of thought begins its other chapter,
I hope I'll get things right in life.

I've had that chance to be someone I could not be
But chose myself instead,
I had that choice between two poles
And picked the one I knew best,
Tomorrow brings new gifts of emotions
And harmonies with a new ocean.

A change of scenery will rest my weary mind
From all the images I thought were left behind,
It's been nearly a month,

A month of what happened
Yet still I have not forgotten,
It's been nearly 3 years since we first met,
The hardest day will come,
Until then I'll play a drum
Hoping for a rhythm as clear as a heartbeat
Beating in perfect motion,
Tomorrow I'll see another ocean,
A change of scenery will rest my mind
From a previous life I left behind.

My cup is now empty
It will be that way for some time,
Until another words out a rhyme
And fills it up again,
But that will be a while yet,
There are things that I must do for myself,
Not for you.

The metal tracks are littered with rocks,

I'm sitting on a moving tube

Waiting for my next stop,

The journey has begun both in my mind

In my life,

For a week I will forget my worries

And set sights on a different ocean

With no notion to what

Weather awaits.

This change of scenery will cause my energy to

Flow in a different space,

I will leave behind the race of constant struggle

7 till 4 always more

Hours upon hours

Until I can't take the stress and tests and figures

With names and numbers.

23.39 a time that seems so long ago,

Now its 10.07,

Seconds will pass then it will be 10.11

Then what after that?

I swig a bottle of sugary liquid

Smiling as I smoke a cigarette.

This journey makes me feel fulfilled,

Like the travellers of old,

I only have to drag my feet,

Let my mind fold,

Wander and think,

More drink.

Beautiful women walk on by,

Charity folk shuffle about,

My eyes follow them both,

But inside I am not devout,

No money in my pocket,

No means to live,

I must wait two days

To receive my wage,

Until then I can relax,

And watch the waves roll back.

Green trees and yellow fields,

Meandering canals and pockets

Of lakes roll on past in my train

As it shakes and rocks gentle

With a jittery caress,

Can't sleep in this mess.

It's 13.50, I'm still drifting to that place

Where situations will be different,

Towers of metal attached by wires

Fly by in an open field,

I can see the beauty of life

Through my small glass window.

I can see the spoils of man

With every fence strung along by

Barbed wire.

I begin to tire.

Deep thoughts.

The pen is caught

In the quaking of the train,

Music floods my brain.

It's becoming hard to sustain

A Deluge of Thoughts

The evening was chaos,
The sky flashed an eerie blue,
Followed by Thor's uncouth growl,
I stalked the early hours through the pavements
When my ears apprehended a howl,
It struck the fear of Fenrir into my heart,
I was ready to follow into the void,
Plummeting so far beneath the Earth.

Now I'm relaxed in a vast ceramic room,
Surrounded by faces in an oceanic haze,
Who are they? I wonder,
Are they awaiting their impending doom?
Will they fail in the achievements
They falsely portray?
Or are they simply waiting for an answer,
That curious wonder to

Come spiralling into their
Naïve minds, leaving all logic falling behind?

A scent ferments from my clothing,
Tonight's antics resting in my breast,
The smell will address all
Of those who pass me by,
I pay no heed to their contradictory thoughts,
I'll be carried on a cloud
Aloft to the philosophy on high.

Silence.
Unadulterated soothing silence,
Ghostly, spiritual, I'm bathing in the literature,
Figures from many cultures converse in strange
Lucid languages and I feel proud
To be a part of this.

Now the deluge has come settling on this city,
Emigrating from above,

I'm engulfed in its shadow
Burdened by its effect,
I'm finding it strenuous to stand evolved, erect.
Feeling more like a barbaric monstrosity,
Shuffling through the alluvium
Of a biblical proportion,
I inspected the celestial sphere
Gazing upon an ancient god's voltaic spear.

In comfort and radiance
You took my hand and squeezed,
Your soft vocals floating on an oral breeze,
I remembered the time we parted ways,
We had been smoking then,
I'll tell you now it left me paranoid and afraid.

In those days when we shared company,
We made an abode from ignorance,
Living in perfect harmony,
It exists in the past

Within the dead eyes of my consciousness,

Released in minimal doses,

Reminding me on occasions,

Leaving the realms of my eyes

Salty and viscous.

"They look like Charles Manson victims"

I heard you speak,

Standing next to me,

I snapped back to the moisture of reality,

Lost in a damp mist,

Warping my rationality,

This deluge of thoughts escaping me.

A Dark Musing

I talk to myself now and again,
Thoughts rambling out of my mouth
Like a piano being dropped from a crane,
Crashing into the silence of doubt.

Secret emotions, manic thoughts and suicide
Are only a passing flirtation of mine,
A trifle to prove my mind is unkind,
Selfish feelings that begin to unwind.

I am a schizo klepto bipolar maniac,
I am a lost generation materializing from the fade,
Some kind of weird creature
Of an acidhead's flashback,
A scientist daydreaming in the shade.

One answer is for sure:

I'm trapped within my head,

Clammy palms pushing on moist spongy doors,

Feet weighed down like lead.

For all my weaknesses, for all my flaws,

My libido is on like a fire escape alarm,

Don't fall for my charm, it is only fake,

A charade designed to make your heart quake.

Sliced

Storm in a raid

Tripoli Decayed

As snubbed civilians

Died facing Polar Bears

With Horatio name tags

Crisscrossed hags

Of rebellious regimes

Torturing tropical storms

Over Yeovil

As Ninjas patrol the streets

And commanders die

In embassies

Fletcher killed Irene

On the UK shores

Tearing apart blitzkrieg memories

Transitions talk

Dictators walk

Out of bubbles

Rubber bullets

In a Moby Dick showcase

While Beasts in Sligo

Wander for 238 dubbed years

In Paedophile Jails

Listening to hounds wail

Rockefeller died

The nefarious albino

Fried in the oils

Of Bernie Nurses

Hangovers lavish

Five million pound weddings

Arctic attacks you have been dreading

It is sexist to question

How you raise your children

You take the stage

In helmet and bullet proof vest

Ready to protest

Your demeaning outrage

Sir

Your indomitable Mother

Gave an account

Of your blazing temper

A dramatic rescue of your soul

Her story to be told

To an audience spanning

33 degrees of rotting flesh

Who Died

Who Died

Who Died

Now the traffic lights

Turn into a rubicund

Chief of Olympian grandeur

As heartbroken fathers

9 a piece

Tattooed tears

On the face

Of independent abortions

Before carrying out counselling

In the clinics

Of escaped murderers.

Coffee Shop Dreams

Sat outdoors in the warming

Radiance of our star,

Indulging in Burroughs'

Twisted sensibility,

Rummaging through change,

Shrapnel in my pocket,

Odd price tag

Glaring at me with pink sobriety.

Casting my mind back,

14 years old,

Obsessed with The Times

Because I thought Starbucks

Was for intellectuals,

Foolish child,

I'm not suitable

For suit and tie

Neck & collar
Wiling away the hours
For a British dollar.

Instead,
10 years later
10 years later
I became obsessed with
Literature,
Literature that twisted the self,
Twisted the eyes
That could twist a geld.

Burroughs, Kerouac, Ginsberg,
How you inspired me,
Tragic remarks,
Tragic philosophy.

Voices moaning,
Voices whispering,

Voices distant in the commercial

Concrete peat,

Hearing snippets of conversations,

My inner voices screaming:

"What is this enchanting mess?"

Realising reality is naught but a test

To restrain our ideology,

Causing evolutionary proctology,

A rectal cancer

On the faces of council bred youth,

Feeding bread to malicious ducks

On parks where festering

Teenagers fuck

Without protection

And plant life Fuck

In an A-Sexual manner,

While I endeavour on sanity's

Decaying edge.

Buildings are Picasso paintings,

Geometric splashes,

Tangerine metro-sexual souls,

Wandering,

Wondering,

Question marking their vanity

With bleached blond domes.

Diamond pierced lobes,

Pathetic nightclub ringtones,

Living for that skull fucking weekend,

Humanity has come to an end.

Good riddance,

For I took that roller coaster downwards

To a bitterly marked spirituality,

Threading my ability

To keep my poetry steady.

In the departure lounge:

"17:21 to Brighton platform 3,"

Not my train,

Not waiting for a train,

Waiting for a body,

Her body,

Female form,

To take with me and make my own

In darkened rooms

And rocking seats,

In night vision halls,

Hoping she admits defeat,

Wanting me forever more.

All I care

All I care

All I care,

Weather is fair,

Dreams are not,

Because I forgot

Where I left my damned clock.

Visions of Aegir

Monsters seen through

The skyscrapers fleeing,

Japanese digital audio

Pissing away shifting

Angry vultures,

Budweiser shots through brutish

Glass bulb serenades,

Orgasms in breeding rectal

Mucus bleeding

Screaming fungus.

Transvestite plumbers working

Hard in the fields

Of lounging potatoes,

Drifting suave machines that

Spill oil on a misjudged plasmatic

Neurological septum,

Pride devouring lust
In nonsensical rhyme.

Porcelain dolls haunting
Frosted remnants of a dull
Sabbatical swimming
Saluting sorrowful quest
In high octane deliverance,
While Norse mythology
Roams these lands
With twisted peasant youth.

Velociraptors make a savage
Pilgrimage across the northern
Territories of Guatemala.

Back in the day we knew
Console game graphics
Were just mannequin plasticine
Rudimentary figures,

Blocks of ash crushed by the
Constraints of time.

I saw Reptiles gnashing chomping
At the excrement of vital organisms,
Bacterial infections
Of humanity's suit of leather
Bound frailties,
Kill me.
Stone dead.

I'm a hallucination in your head,
A dream of a dream trapped
Within a night terror,
Threat level heightened,
Frightened of the insatiable
Bogeyman to launch like
Apollo 11 into your
Satellite imaginations.

Waters are like amber nectar,

Rivers of honeycomb sweetness,

Lavishing sweetened seductions

Dressed in comforted

Pyjama bottoms,

Loathing temptations,

Cold calculated distress,

Adoring dawns blooming majesty,

Suffering brittle calcium

Of a Lithuanian Christian charity.

(Religion is false) it says,

How can God be truth

If falsified accusations

Deter the speech of scripts

Laid down by philosophical priests?

Answer?

I guess not.

Fairy tales died in pixie dust swamps,

While fishermen pondered
The spawning nature of kelp.

Furniture burned at the stakes
Of consumer wealth,
Literature burned at the gates of industry,
Nature yearned for Apple's nursery.

The shape of L,
While the Cure perform Love Cats
In basement Marijuana hazed rooms,
Heaving spliffs,
Packed joints,
Smoke rings breaking the seal
Of a magical foretold doom.

Crowley appeal to me,
Find me in goat farms
Attached to horns
Sexualized by bisexual

Nymph maid Fawns.

Insects prowl
Before maggots crawl,
Worms ride filth
Into anal churches
That respond to our calls.

Noir pioneers saw it all
Through broken glass,
Through broken statues
And broken constitutions,
Commanding chains, guys talking,
Watch commander
Trusting instincts to police,
Apologies in uniform solidarity.

"Let's face it, things were better
In the '60s when Negros
Were slaves in movies

And Injuns were old and grey,"
He spoke with confidence,
This nonce of fashion and travesty,
Ignorant, waiting, dormant,
Circumstantial combinations
Of psychiatrists
And mammalian aliens.

Cyborg centipedes elegantly
Swim through the maple syrup
Of Fort Knox,
Beauty, the beauty of money,
Enticing colours of fruity
Sour grapefruit,
Pink bitter amnesty.

The fading sun is setting,
The sky is ablaze,
Grey pillars of smoke,
The fires of another world,

The crashing waves: Aegir's anguish,

While mortals gaze upon

Its raw awe inspiring beauty,

Take me there,

Carry humanity afar,

Distil our stagnant lives,

A molten stain across the heavens,

With ripples of lava delight,

Viewing sponge skies through

Reddened eyes.

Even Dreams Can't Hide Emotions

The Crustaceans

That transmogrified

Into resplendent daughters

Of the maritime antiques

Caused me to spasm

In wrenching orgasm,

Putrid secreting concubines

Laid in abundance

Smooth azure eggs.

Nine seconds pass,

These aquatic cackle berries

Form baroque scales,

Obscure and divine,

Eleven seconds pass

Now they begin to hatch,

The top twists off like

A jam jar lid
Out spring these
Misshapen fruits.

Tomatoes with Human faces!
Oranges with Feline faces!
Apples with Canine faces!
An eerie kiwi with my face
Protrudes from its malachite flesh!

So I'm isolated on this island,
No friends, lonely,
Buried in this existence
In a subterranean void,
My memories slowly become sand,
No family, lonely,
Dreams are my only poetry
Told through late nights
Ending in glazed afternoons
Where pen meets paper,

Allowing my imagination take flight.

If I move back home,
Back with my family,
I would feel complete,
But would miss this island,
I would have to sign on
At the job centre in Dudley
And live in a room
Where I have no privacy.

But the sinking feeling
Within my chest cavity
Tells me I'm missing something,
Something vital,
Maybe it's just fleeting, trivial,
From the loneliness I feel,
In desperation
I need to remedy.

Simple words,

Simple emotions,

Simple solitude

Drifting on time's oceans.

The Sirens pursued,

I could hear the schlep, schlep, schlep

Of moist tail fin on concrete

As they gained.

"There's a battle within my mind,

What I want and what I need,

A conflicting charade

That will not take heed

Of what my heart can't find,"

I cry out in a pathetic squeak.

Pathetic, yes that's me,

Trapped inside this damp bubble,

In a log cabin by a seductive lake,

Its diamond surface shimmering

In the autumn phosphorescence,

Reflecting the redwood, pine and oak,

My peers being kidnapped

Choked in this paradise,

While I, helpless, breathed insanely

For the tragedy of Pompeii.

Irrelevant? Maybe so,

But my mental state

Isn't comfortable

In this realm because

Even dreams can't hide emotions,

No matter how cryptic they seem to flow.

Sixty-five

The coffee touched his lips,

Like a dramatic encore

He took another sip,

Then paused to recall the night

Where fires burned

And Angels screamed.

The theme of a naked city

Is always black & white,

And he knew what it meant

To be beckoned to a convent

Of pagan nuns

Of witchdoctors

Of any type of cult that would take him in.

Sixty-five: a number that thrived

Within his mind,

Trapped in repetitive momentum,

Manifesting his destiny

With every filament,

He'll soon become

An existential entity,

Lying dormant in a world of crazy,

Wallowing in fantasies awfully decadent.

The world was painted

With sedimentary rock,

With cretaceous pride

(Sixty-five)

And he stepped out

Into the Midwestern morning

With his dreams redefined.

Numerology beckoned his

Best abilities

And expanded them

With viral agility,

He stepped into time

(Sixty-five)

Thus, prophesising the end of time.

The river glimmered

In the winter sun

As he waded in,

The sensation,

Like a billion needles,

Made him shiver,

He felt like a beacon transmitting to God.

"Where is my lord?"

He spoke in outer body delirium,

"For I have foreseen that the end is nigh!"

When no answer comforted him

He perceived it as a sign,

And in Lyssa's embrace he would die,

Fixated on God's abandonment,

Another fading lullaby.

His war with God
Would begin in the mountains
Of clouds that surrounded heaven,
At the gates he raised his sword
And with fire he would bring down
The Lord's reign.

The omnipotent One consulted him,
Seeing the bravery of this mortal soul,
Taking pity on the man's twisted mind,
He baptised him as a brother:
"No longer shall we be at war,"
God spoke unto to this man,
"For I will always be on your side
When you fight in my Holy Name."
The All Powerful One
Refrained from thundering laughter,
A cruel joke was played on this soul,
That hung from heaven's rafters.

Then he, brought back from Death's stutter,

Rose from his grave in a field of peyote,

Enacted justice on the wicked and unjustly,

Slaughtering innocent lives

(Sixty-five)

Because in his mind he was saintly,

Doing the work of the Lord so holy,

But in reality, just a modern-day Don Quixote,

With unnatural violent tendencies.

Sixty-five minutes after his revival,

He was bludgeoned in the brain

And sent straight down to hell,

Left to wallow in his crazed shame,

Without a story to tell,

The wits of his soul the Devil did cull,

Turning him into a bestial demon,

Another member of that hellish hive,

Chanting the fateful number,

Sixty-five.

Sixty-five.

Sixty-five.

An Intoxicated Note

The foundations of us and who we are,

Mixed in with consciousness

And thickened black tar,

Brought feelings of grief when I was on leave,

With literary notes stuffed up my sleeve,

And figures of your love viewed from afar.

The things we said brought suffering

In both our heads, it all means nothing

In the vast expanse of life,

So, lend me a lyric from a song we adore

And sing it with all our verbal gore.

I saw Cthulhu in the clouds

Timing his appearance in the heavens,

Air conditioners rasped their cool, stale voice,

I chased you in my dreams,

Descriptions I care not to mention.

The brittle calcium of our acquaintance
Shattered into ivory dust,
Then freaks of knitted jumpers
Made note of my dismissal
When they discovered my trivial lust.

An intoxicated note
From yesterday evening's bottle,
When I capsized off the moon,
Take this poem as gospel,
Lay me to rest with Neptune,
All I deserve is that mildew aroma,
When I crossed your unequivocal moat,
And floated down your forbidden river.

Aquatic Apathy

Bury me in aquatic reeds,

When desert farms

Are engulfed by the seas,

I've been cleansed in

Atmospheric dysentery,

With unprovoked charm,

There is no-one,

Only me.

I once slew my soul

Replaced it with bigotry,

The critters gained control,

There I slept and wept,

I kept pushing,

Forces repelling this organic engine.

Swamped with notes,

Manuscripts of rationalisation,
Deducing the equations,
Nurturing the contingents
Of my inebriating industry,
Spreading the illiterate virus
With paralyzing veracity.

"Breathing in the shoals
Far beneath the roads,
While my brain decodes
Fortune's revealing ode."

Desperation clipped me
With impeccable precision
With its bullet of damnation,
Time seemed to glisten
On a distant island,
Travelling on the breeze,
The resonance of a violin.

My heart accompanied,

The music haunted

With its tender beat,

The cryptic shackles

Of this lament

I wanted fused on repeat.

Bury me in

Homorhythmic bedlam,

When reality

Has become quantum,

To be cleansed in

Nature's chivalry,

With tranquil oiled apathy.

Apocrypha

Broken scars

Across the evening sky,

Streaked like infant tears

I lay my bed in the marshes

With the ancient mayfly,

Wiping my lucidity clear.

Humanity gave up

With a whimper

Over the long stretch of time,

Now out of the ebony sky

Comes rolling thunder,

They thought their caliginous actions

To be sublime.

No thoughts,

No voices fled from within,

Just stupefied silence

That was much akin

To the minds of the muted ignorant,

My monologue speaking absent,

About their ancient bold doctrine

Falling on deaf ears

Leaving my breath to stiffen.

I wandered across the

Strange path of this reality,

Witnessed time with

Heightened sense of ability,

I hope one day to return

To that lurid world

Where imagination is serenely hurled

Into a vat of potent delight,

Where friends and foes

Can love deeply into the night.

The leaves are falling now

Across autumn's sunburst skies,

I'm perched on this hill
Harkening humanities silent outcry,
Feeling a chill crawl
Tentatively up my back,
The urge to flee gripping me.

Let me journey
Far from this province,
Let me catch a glimpse
Of the constellations.
Let me discover
A natural path to convince
My consciousness of its emancipation.

On the road I saunter
Through bramble and bush,
The crystal ice of winter's chill
Breathing my cheeks to a scarlet flush,
There are few who chose to survive,
Many that chose to die,

Those of us left are all alone,
Our last breath before the plunge.

The words of mine,
Like the words of others,
Went unheard,
Lying awake under the black veil
I pondered, feeling blurred
About the slow intoxication
Of our spirituality,
Scream my pain tonight with me,
Cough up the phlegm
From the polluted moon
Where the dead were sent
And callously strewn.

One day I will give up,
Exhaustion taking me
Into her arms,
For I have witnessed

Too much depravity,

Like the whore's that work

On their decadent farms,

Now I will rest my eyes,

Feeling bleary,

Tomorrow I push on,

An unknown goal leaving no boundary.

Let me journey

Far from this province,

Let me catch

A glimpse of the constellations.

Let me discover

A natural path to convince

My consciousness of its emancipation.

Electric squalls lick

The shores of the heavens,

Like a tsunami bound

For its destiny,

I meditate underneath

This cosmic beacon,

Feeling at peace,

Shrouded by the barley.

21st Century Prehistoric Revival

I have been waiting since Judea's time,
I crossed the canyons of prehistoric lines,
I felt the sweat of fossilised brutes,
Chiming a tune from their Precambrian Lutes.

The palaeontologist's looped vinyl spoke:
"Digging, digging, digging beast!
When the reptiles rise you shall be free,
Blood orgies and flesh tearing feasts!"

This is a revival of Stone Age glory,
Taking wing in amorous country,
I stole your innocence efficiently,
Always seizing the merciless opportunity.

21st Century voluptuous female,
You glanced at me whilst smashing shale,

Your lotus brought combusting desires,
Make love to me in this hypocritical satire.

My ugly sins are my art,
Don't impose or try to thwart,
There are miracles to be found in the desert,
Should you discover them you'll find no comfort.

Drug abuse and alcohol consumption,
Skulking in towns like a lost gunman,
Drawing to fire at modern day laws,
Another Aphrodite sub clause.

In Nevada the wolves approached the shade,
Their law on the land must be obeyed,
I dragged my bounty of women to a cage,
Where the hounds will feast in bloody rage.

The stage has now been set,
I have never felt regret,

For my primal urges and neurosis,

I will wallow in the wilderness with my hubris.

An Ejaculation of Words

Pulsating through a cosmic intestine,
A Melton Mowbray phantom
Encased in jelly jizzum,
Spat from the protective bowels
Into this harsh terrain,
Covered in the sticky residue
Of a thousand procreations.

A Truth So Simple

Boreas breathe your cotton sheath
Of winters first chill onto me as I make
These streets my shelter for a while,
The homeward journey
Speaks as an autumn leaf
Cradled by the seasons changing arms.

Go down the meandering lane,
Soon it will go,
Stealing my emotions,
Seeing it all pass away.

The cars are empty husks,
I have seen enough,
A shift in pattern
Where Notus claimed
The branches of dying trees,

Where is that piano?
The one that soothed
The cabins of my dreams.

I want it now,
Maybe it will be gone tomorrow,
I want it to be gone,
Like the alien sounds
Of my nervous sorrow.

The motorways are deserted,
A mist settles, frozen,
The glassy concrete hurts
My softly bound feet
They are so alone,
I sigh alone.

I sat by the fire that burned low
In the cosmic womb,
Mother night,

Bear me into your sleeping bosom,
Bring me an orchestra to
Build those dreams into a crescendo.

You shall know,
All that I came to know,
I am coming home,
A truth so simple,
You will follow,
Sensual Theremins
Whisper images,
Returning to my door.

I never wanted more,
Only this moment with you,
I'm returning to my shores,
To be by the fire with you.

Theatre Dreamer

Control the temporal flow
With a telekinetic banjo,
Strumming a psychotic cello
Down in the dense Congo,
You've always relished the chase.

Sleep, child, dream
Your death will break the seams,
Illusionary rhymes reign supreme,
Pulsating within your bloodstream,
Sanity, misplaced.

I have given you all,
My soul, my black book,
My undesired teacher taught
How to dress souls
In pretty bows

And dolphin diamonds,
A break in the poem
Shows I mean business
When you witness
My fabled, flawless
Theatre dreamer.

Debt collectors, red letter
Telephone babbler,
Low income is your anchor,
Setting goals with this cancer,
Don't you want reality erased?

"Bringing in the sheaves"
A song dedicated to me?
You find it hard to believe
This prophecy I did conceive,
Time is out of place.

The masses have congregated

To pay homage

To the loathing of humanity's

Segregated attitudes,

That makes the malice mills

Turn wheels of burning greed,

And your chants only feed

Brutal pigs that wallow

In faecal matter brimming with puss,

What? You thought your actions were just?

Paranoid laughter

For your monetary enchanter,

Mankind's biographical author,

Cocaine and hookers,

Snake eyes on reality's dice.

The pavements turn to steam,

Your conscience cannot be redeemed,

It may sound bitterly extreme

In the grandest of schemes,

Guess it will have to suffice.

Fly to the stars,
Crawling on the carpet,
Jacked up on fleeting memories,
Past, present, future,
Misrepresented companies
Of artistic values,
Tis time oh paupers
To rabble and ramble,
Hold those banners up high,
Your time has come to comply!

Sanity misplaced,
You always loved the chase,
I've always given you
My soul,
Gravity shifts, wailing in the mist,
Time is always out of place.

A Fading Lullaby

Fading lullabies,
Swaying in the dawn sky,
Imprinting melodies,
Enough to make the dusk shy.

See the envy of the storm,
Readying to break formation,
Breathing in anticipation,
Within the cogs of imagination.

Dripping down the cross,
Through oceans of time,
What I thought I had lost
Was just a chiming sign
From the distant coastline,
Sailing on shores, through silenced halls.

Drifting through your palace,
Upon the dirt of the world,
The markings of a man, ageless,
And stories left untold.

See the envy of the storm,
Readying to break formation,
Screaming in anticipation,
Upon the gears of emancipation.

Tangled within the web of destiny,
Golden waterfalls of the mind,
Eyes staring, haunting and glassy,
Under faces I can't define,
Those distant squalls leaving me blind.

See the envy of the storm,
Readying to break formation,
Knowing your anticipation,
Is leading to an unknown destination.

When Life Takes A Bollock

I allowed myself to slip away
Into the gray haze,
Where my future resides,
Alternative worlds behind the eyes,
Running through the night,
My inexorable demise in sight.

It's melodramatic,
But the diagnosis was hypnotic,
My mind tends to wander,
Symbiotic thoughts trying to barter
With logic, it doesn't work.

Shock is the first emotion,
My devotion to life fades,
A notion of being cast into the shade.
These pompous words

Cannot describe the true feelings
One experiences from this news,
Like I am dreaming,
In pursuit of the waking world.

There is a scar that is rarely seen,
But I feel it every day,
The aches, the phantom pain,
The remnants of organic tissue,
I will never be the same.

Life continues as it always has,
And I am forced to live it,
A shattered shell,
Clothed in pretend razzmatazz,
Living in my own private hell.

I digress and must confess
These feelings are not constant,
They are merely fleeting moments,

Snippets of resting sentiments.

For the most part I am fine,

But five years is such a long time

To be scrutinized,

Every test result reprised,

My fears revised,

If my life is suddenly re-modified.

My mortality stroked me,

My heart turned to stone,

I'm flying above a chasm,

Chasing the phantasm of myself,

Through an existential crisis I roam,

While serenely the world churns

And I secretly yearn for normality,

But mortality stroked me,

My fate forever unknown.

In seconds one can feel a plethora of emotions,

A dynamic cocktail, a path to oblivion.

My moods are subtle transitions,
Those alternate worlds, mere reflections,
Because when life takes a bollock
I gain clarification, a whole new interpretation
Of this fragile and fugitive existence.

Sedgley

Sedgley,
It echoes in my heart,
Oscillates through my arteries,
Vibrates like a symphony,
This town and I in matrimony,
A place to lay my lifeless body.

Images of its roads and scars across its fields,
I remember sometime in late December
How friends and I would
Scamper around the streets with booze,
Underage we were pursued by the police,
We fled in drunken jovial moods,
Our private teenage festivities.

I wasn't born here but definitely bred,
I grew up in the shadow of the Beacon,
A tower of stone used for astronomy,

It always provided a temporary
Home for those who couldn't make amends
With their broken families.

Ecstasy, cannabis, cocaine and speed,
Marching through the streets
We plodded and ploughed
With rolling eyes and gurning mouths,
Past hallucinations in our minds,
Memories hard to summarize,
Engaging in confused chatter
And philosophical rhyme.

I moved away, a long time ago,
I didn't know what else to do,
But after years of being alone
I long to return to all of you,
In Sedgley,
To break the isolation,
Where my heart can finally be free.

Imperfect lives and imperfect people,
Those whom I love slowly dwindle
Into a past I struggle to remember,
It's a part of growing older,
Nothing ever lingers.

Despite these morose musings
Sweet memories neutralise the corrosive,
My hometown will never be imposing,
For no matter where I go
The circle will always close here,
I am the rambling fellow
Who will die in Sedgley,
This town I will always revere.

Afternoon Window

Mist,

Lingering above the ocean,

The ships pass by like ghosts,

The island is a silhouette

Shrouded in mysteries.

She sits on my lap

Blocking the view

Of the glistening waters,

I don't mind.

We kiss.

She has pink flowers

In her hair.

Seagulls fight over food,

The remnants of barbecues,

Clusters of people remain,

Beer is drunk,

I can hear distant conversations

And laughter,

Banter.

My afternoon window is stained,

But the views remain the same:

Divine.

The world is divine,

And the lady on my lap is divine.

Her eyes shine.

Winner of Editor's Poem of the Day on The Poetry Forum: 30th March 2012.

Kinetic Dreams

Hush in her sound,
I stand in between,
Pushed by the mouth,
I see her it's been too long.
Oh so long.

Falling from Heaven
On infinite clouds,
She brought me flowers
In the cosmic shroud.

Kinetic dreams,
Falling in between
Mountains of the mind
That I must climb,
Mathematic morsels
On the rocks of time,

Speaking in rhyme
From the distant coastline.

Waking and dreaming,
Waking and screaming,
I cannot see her,
It's been too long,
Where did it go wrong?
The threads of our union
Spun so strong
Then weakened by delusions.

Technology gleamed
From the binary oceans,
I began to perceive
Her translucent motion,
I'm drifting apart
From the crutch of this realm,
Those fading scars
Are beginning to meld,

With the fabric of my being.

Every fabric of my being.

Dirt on the Bones

The muscles rippled
Like sonic waves in sand,
While the body swayed
Like bluebells in the breeze,
The legs find it difficult to stand.

The hands are forced
To clean up the mess,
Left behind like the wounds
I won't redress.
The eyes witness light
Diminishing; the setting sun,
The toes feel rocks in dust
In the desert.

There is litter here
The mind registers pollution,

Bags tumbling
Like spools of wicker,
Admiration of the devotion,
Paranoia staring at the reflection.

Signalling danger
At the patterns in the dirt,
Those hands begin to hurt,
Those muscles begin to tear,
Those eyes sting from the sweat
Dripping from the hair.

The hole has not yet been dug,
Already the vultures gather,
Necks bent like the spine
As the body pulls and pulls and pulls,
And slump, in it goes,
The lungs are relieved,
The package has been received
By the earth

The dirt fills the void,
But still I am paranoid
When looking at my reflection.

It's another transition,
A metamorphosing delusion,
Another blackout will occur,
Another hole will be dug.

Malfunction

I run to you but
I've no reason to pursue
An ancient memory.
My thoughts revert to you,
Knowing our moments were few
On this island I now inhabit.

Our love was an inkjet
Malfunctioning at its end,
A symphony of lasers
Cutting through our defense,
I can still smell the wounds,
Those searing wounds.

Jittery

The ligaments connecting my sanity
Have snapped.
I'll tap till my breath runs flat.
The breeze is full of coffee aromas,
That bedazzle my sovereignty
To tempt me into handing over my novelty,
Making me dumb and blind.

A bell chimes in the crowd,
Audible land mines astound tourists,
Never leave your cloaks at home,
People don't want to see your naked emotions,
Keep them embedded in your tomes
So the words can be inscribed inside your tombs.

In the shade it is cold,
But I feel too old to wander around

In the sunshine where I don't belong.

My ramblings save me from cracking.

Skin on my feet, cracking.

My eyes will dry, cracking.

My mind is high, cracking.

Not going to crack,

Listen to the footsteps,

The clomping heels

And relax.

And a dog barks,

Jittery little fucker sets me off.

In my head I'm a murderer,

Horrific fantasies that could make you shudder.

In the Sun it is warm,

I feel safe beneath its rays,

Though my skin will burn

And flake away.

My urges subside,

Stay away from the shade.

Scuttle

I got spooked on the dark esplanade
Instead of filling me with a sense of security
The patches of amber light only served to fill me
With more dread.
I saw something scuttle
On the shingle shore
And leaped out of my flesh.
It was a seagull unlike no other,
It looked like a miniature-mutated pterodactyl.
I stopped and scrutinized the critter for a while,
Considered its scarred face
And the growth on its back.
Another bird, or a clinging tumour?
I still do not know.
All I know is that it filled me with fear
Then came the crux:
It hobbled sideways like an autistic crab

Flapping its wings.

Its ruffled feathers were covered in blood

Stark rouge patches that stood

Out amidst the amber lamplight.

Poor little bastard,

Who, or what, would do such a thing?

I knew I had to escape the esplanade

Before I suffered a similar fate.

Sixtus

"Feast on bones in your kingdom of fear,

A bag of demons in your eyes my dear."

Curtains produced succulent flowers

Which expelled pollen

Carried by bee-like bats

With conscious personalities

Who fed their swarms of fertile children

With bowls of nutty yogurt

Frothing with rabies

Snapping with crazy nonsense

Whether they should rejoice

At the clenching arseholes

Who stared with constipated misery

Shifting uncomfortably

In the foetus chambers

Prepared by swallows charged on caffeine

Bringing garish dreams into the fray

On cloudy days

Shaking down the people

With gut wrenching cries

Leaving all around the infinite scenarios

So that they could collide with each other

Melding the acts together

With the glue of words.

Without You

Being without you,

It's like staring into the abyss,

All I see is eternal void,

A lifetime of darkness,

It threatens to consume my being.

I am afraid if you don't accept my heart,

It will fill me with its self-realising emptiness,

The abyss will flow through,

That is what it's like,

Being without you.

Transitions

I'm still searching for a life,

A confession, a transition,

To transport me from it all,

I'm always looking for more,

A nonchalant response,

An endless cycle,

Looping like a noose

Around my existence,

I'm nothing to you

And nobody to myself,

These poems represent a repetition

Within my soul,

Flaunting abstract jargon,

Craving more,

There must be more,

This can't be it

This is not living how I see fit.

Another confession, another transition.

My body is a ghost ship

Lacking life, no morsels of humanity,

Can you blame me

For feeling so empty?

I'm told to keep it simple,

Keep it sweet,

Keep it consistent,

Altogether something neat.

I find it hard to sleep,

These days are complex,

Finding the desire to believe

In myself, in me,

In my future, is difficult,

Drifting, disillusioned,

Too many confessions,

Too many transitions.

There is no victory,

There is no achievement,

There is no poetry,

Only my penchant

For transitioning,

For always questioning

The world inhabiting around me.

Painful Literature

My prayers are empty pleas
That debase all forms
Of religious ceremony,
I am hollow like
The brittle shells of peanuts,
Scattered across the land,
Scorned for my loneliness,
But I demand it.
This is no time for
The jovial company
Of companions,
Or even their dramatic pity,
This is time
For solitary confinement
On my own
Cancer stricken continent.
Tears were like a flash flood

Flowing from my eyes,

So weary of looking

At this tired life around me,

Instead of taking

Solace in comfort

I favoured the linoleum floor

Instead of my bed,

There I shed salty moisture,

Convulsing in desperation,

Trying to clutch

Onto some form of hope.

I found a chasm betwixt

My soul and flesh,

In it stirred something

Putrid and alien,

Something with a mind

Made to meddle in human affairs,

Taking lives without consequence,

How could such a thing evolve

From nature's bosom?

Curses spewed from my mouth,

After mere minutes

Of this debacle I calmed,

Collected the fragments

Of my mental state

And pieced them back together

As best I could,

This puissant disease

Is the author of my final chapter,

What I would give to erase

And rewrite such painful literature.

You Weren't Happy

I am uninspired,

Because my mind is swollen

With nine to five banality,

My muse has been stolen from me,

All because you said you weren't happy,

With me, with yourself,

Those promises we made

Left to decay on the shelf

Of another memory

That fades into the grey void

Between you and me.

The past six months are now dead,

The future we had planned

Is now crumbling like a castle

Built in miserable sand,

And now I'm left barren

Of all inspiration,

Unsure of where my emotions stand

In this constant battle with you.

It happened unexpectedly,

Your sincerity slicing like a blade

Twisting my guts, severing our love,

Would you snap a dove's neck

If it landed on your shoulder?

In this uncertainty, I am afraid,

Then slowly our memories

Begin to moulder.

I keep dreaming about you,

It's not right for my mind to assume

These paranoid visions,

Jealous transitions through

Unvisited dimensions,

A vat of false information

As I flounder in my rotten emotions,

An ocean of corpses,
A bloated metamorphosis
Inflating my brains like a blowfish.

I have to prick myself on barbs
To awaken from these visions,
An ambition to make myself
Surface from this perdition
I have designed through abandonment
Because I am no longer wanted
For a future
For a family
All because you said you weren't happy,
Now I'm not happy,
And in this mutual unhappiness
We find ourselves free
At a price we paid too dearly.

Beyond My Office Window

In the early morning,
When the usual staff were just
Memories of the past and
Waiting ghosts of the future,
The theatre was all but silent.
The old building creaked,
The wind outside rushed
Through miscellaneous cracks
And vents and caused doors
To open and close with
Ghostly suddenness.
My ears played tricks on me,
Phantom footsteps and voices
Carried on the wind from the world
Beyond the antediluvian walls
Gave the illusion of a building
Haunted by the apparitions of

All who had trodden the

Crimson carpet of long ago.

The passing traffic beyond my

Office window reminded me

That I wasn't trapped in a vortex

Of spirits clambering to make

My acquaintance.

There were only the doldrums

Of another gloomy day and

Now I was the apparition

Risen from the early morning clay

To haunt my colleagues

And the guests who stay

For a show,

To be entertained and forget

Their silent sorrow,

Those who straddle the streets

As above, so below where they can't see

My lurking glow,

Out beyond my office window.

What I Saw on Duty

Knelt on the pavement,

A vagrant in khaki trousers

And camo print coat

Fumbled with a pair of headphones

In a rainwater moat,

Bright orange wires,

Tangled, as he studied them

With ape-like curiosity,

His filthy hands turned the device

In concise movements,

Deliberate primitive devotion

Caught in his eyes,

Handling a timeworn tool

Of shale

Instead of a modern implement.

His head twitched,

There were grunts of frustration

As the fascination dissipated

Into a bubbling primeval rage,

Sounds erupting from his toothless mouth,

As he tried to untangle the wires bound

About his sickly smeared hands.

I observed this with the attitude

Of a child at a zoo,

This primordial figure seemed not to

Care about the rain soaking his clothes,

Nestles within his rainwater moat,

More grunts snatching in his throat.

Eventually he loosened the orange cable,

I watched him untangle then wrangle his wits

In a frenzy of triumphant glee,

An indefatigable beast let loose on the streets,

And I barked a laugh and continued with

My duties,

As he leaped up and cursed at his

Damp knees.

I Am More Like Frankenstein

Every lover I lose
I grieve as though they had died,
The stress eats at my heart
And I start to enter a state of mourning,
These emotions breed an intensity
That I choose not to see,
Only ignored until the end,
These relationships briefly
Pass, none of them last,
A handful of months
None surpassing years,
Not for a long time anyway,
I fear my destiny is to be alone,
My chance to atone for all the sex,
All the mess I've made of my life,
All the women I've left behind,
Hearts that I've broken,

Awoken bitterness, created monsters,

My mom calls me Casanova,

But I am more like Frankenstein.

Piecing together memories

Dug from graves in my subconscious,

Lightning bolts of dreams

Decline in the night, I might,

Just might, fall in love again,

Hoping next time my mind refrains

From these fuck ups.

What is so wrong with me?

Can I not see?

Am I the very definition of insanity?

Do they perceive me

As a lunatic lost in his own eccentricity?

Maybe it's true.

Maybe I'm not fit for romantic partnerships,

Perhaps I have been chosen by divinity

To walk alone for the duration of my longevity,

I am constantly in a love longing dilemma,
Wandering lost along my road of time,
My mom calls my Casanova,
But I am more like Frankenstein.

I admit I have abandonment issues,
This could be why I spew confusion
At a situation when they leave me,
Believe me I'd like to move on,
But I have to know the reason why
Before that can happen,
Until then I wallow in self deprecation,
Cursing myself, wondering what I had done
wrong,
A throng of voices in my mind babbling
Ceaselessly, eventually they will go quiet,
To silence them I need to find another
Woman to help me forget the one
Who left me to my devices,
A stigma that rots away my rhyme,

My mom calls me Casanova,

But I am more like Frankenstein.

The Briny Miasma

In the briny froth his fate was sealed,
In blood and foam he made the deal,
To marry flesh with turbulent waters,
No remains left for his sons and daughters.

Tracing the sea with his crimson plasma,
Drowned and shredded in that briny miasma,
As the fantastical fathoms frittered away his soul,
He called out to his mother out there in the vault.

He wished he had tried harder,
He knows that all the fruitless soul searching
On the unforgiving oceans
Drove him to the edge, his sanity broken.

He screamed at the heavens
That were fraught with stormy contemplation:
'Twas my fault for being caught

In the net of my emotions,
Now I shall pay for my nautical devotion.

He leapt into his doom,
Ripped and torn apart,
Liquefied maroon is what he became,
From this land loving world
He did depart, with only himself to blame.

Earthly Insanity Part II

I would rather die

Than be one of those lonely

Banshee wails broadcasting

From the slithers of open windows

In nursing home rooms,

Cast aside by society

To become a malleable piece of putty

At the mercy of malignant hands

While my mind and body

Become maligned by old age

And despair.

I would rather my soul glide

Into the embrace of the Grim Reaper

To bind my soul to his forever

Than suffer just after midnight

Agonising with existential worry

Gut-wrenching cries and loss of memory.

I would rather be free

Where mortality cannot harm me,

Where my plodding steps are just a

Rationality of the mortal soul

Encapsulated in weariness

A journey to make amends

With my past conformity

To every ideology laid bare

And broken before me.

I would rather life be done with me,

So another poor soul can take my place

In this existence where destiny is another

Tragedy of human deviancy

And our ascendency takes place

Upon an example of spiritual probity,

So in that company I will truly be free,

Safe within my earthly insanity.

Abyssal Anxiety

All I am is heaps of bones inside folds of flesh

Tangled in endless entrails and visceral veins,

Ballooned with blood dribbling drearily

Through depressed arteries of thought patterns,

Criss crossed with a brain like moss

Spreading as a fungal infection

Through a rudimentary consciousness

That I cannot contain

Within a natural intelligence.

I am a complicated cadaver,

A mutual lover of the infestations

I call nightmares,

Of dreams that split the seams of my sanity,

Of fantasies that malform the mould

Of simple curiosity,

Of jittery chatter champing cheekily

Across the majesty of my conscious structure.

I am he who observes through orbs that absorb
Every moment every movement every sycophant
Who tries to appease its peers by peering
Into their desires and stoking the fire
Of the lustful denier that they have become
When faced with retribution
Brought on by a vengeful pursuer,
The need to conspire against those they love.

In this bag of blood I watch
And flood myself with a wrath that bubbles
Like beads of foam frothing wearily
A rabid misery and post-modern sobriety,
All in a touch, all in a print, all in ridges
Meant to bring identity and solitary prosperity,
Only delivering amnesty from
Those who perceive me
In a deliberate and maniacal way,

Until they speak a tardy apology,

Releasing me from a prison

Of musings about mental sensitivity

And ruminations regarding seasonal despondency,

All flaunted beneath a wreath

In the solstice of sin,

A life lived within the textures and geometries

Of bygone days, memories recaptured

That can never be delayed,

Trapped in a haze as I wither with age.

So I leave my flesh in a heap of slag

A betrayed rag doped up on

The fickle fragments of

An oracle's ordnance

Where I, so confounded by the words

Breathed onto me,

Are profoundly turned to a gospel of gore

A chore of the body, a burden on the soul,

A goal obtained through pain and lust

Justifying the trust I had in you all,
A grandiose fall into abyssal anxiety,
A condition that will plague me
For all of eternity.

Paper Ghosts

A gang of teenagers,

The harbingers of adolescent angst

Swift as paper ghosts

Drifting on the autumn breeze,

Went biking down the road

With cries of ignorant glee,

Silhouetted by moving machinery

Lights straight from the pages of ufology

To a destination I'll never

Be privy to, but I imagine

To some function of youthful

Depravity, storming the castle

Of conformity with brutal jokes

And cigarette ash, blinding soot

Of centuries worth of uniformity,

Burned to cinders

Like paper ghosts

Drifting on the autumn breeze.

Lonesome man, high vis effigy,

Waiting in line to buy bread and cheese,

A reaper of his own inebriated qualities,

Like a paper ghost

Drowning in treacherous seas,

Puddle of liquid forms at his feet,

Confusion from the cashier at what he sees,

Lonesome man shaking his leg

As liquid sluices down his skin,

Seeps through his joggers,

His glazed eyes blasé, this high vis effigy

Does not retreat, completes his transaction

With a damp and dreary destiny,

Like a paper ghost

Drowning in treacherous seas.

A crooked woman, misshaped

Like a human-velociraptor hybrid,

Flabby, scaly, a wretched survivor

Of a life she lived before prison had claimed her,

Where she was treated as a zoetic disease,

Like a paper ghost

Clinging onto dying trees,

With unbelievable strain she squeezed

Through the gap of a telephone box,

Digging for change with hands riddled with pox,

A grey ragged woman with no natural shame

Fiddled in her knickers with perverse pain,

Rutting animalistic with unnatural ease,

Like a paper ghost

Clinging onto dying trees.

A hypnagogic man, bloodshot eyes

Bulging from his skull,

Mouth wide open full of yellow teeth,

Gums that despise the cigarette he sucks,

Underneath he decays and plucks at dead skin,

As he shucks his feet into an alcoholic pose,

Shuffles in shoes falling apart at the soles,

Bagful of booze, his addiction he must appease,

Like a paper ghost

He was never meant to be.

He breathes heavily

From a mouth that never closes,

His eyes look like fleshy mutated roses,

Opening and closing, focusing on the glamor

The pygmies and the horror,

He collapses in a heap,

Passes away from this life and his crumbling city,

Like a paper ghost,

He was never meant to be.

Single mother with a burden child,

Taunting tantrums in the rain,

It's been this way for a while,

Her spawn plays this game with nothing to gain,

Her knackered pram stutters starts and screams,

Wheels catching on pebbles on Southsea beach,

She stares at the Solent and yearns to be free,

Like a paper ghost

With hollow eyes staring endlessly.

The waves touch the child

A baptism in infanticide,

Up to her waist she wades,

Babe in arms still screeching with bile,

She cannot abide this for all of her days,

It's a moment of madness she chooses not to see,

Like a paper ghost

With hollow eyes staring endlessly.

A faux pharmaceutical

Retributional man storms deplorably

Mind snatched of sensibility

By creeping utterly nefariously

Towards the road of his reckoning,

Flitting through blustering winds,

With his drug dealer swagger,

Drug dealer phone, drug dealer bag

And a bone to pick with customers,

In the icy autumn rain he's likely to freeze,

Like a paper ghost

He is torn apart easily.

Accusations of rape, gearing up for a bar fight,

A coke fuelled maniac,

Trooper of the mid-week night,

His voice is like gravel stern shroud on his face,

Disgraceful behaviour, another demon to chase,

Eyes skittish like a Jesus lizard

Thrice self-proclaimed Pompey lad,

On this sodden Halloween he's a gaunt ghoul

Haunting the southern lands,

Scrubbing his hands that start bleeding profusely,

Breathing through a nose

Littered with ivory scree,

Like a paper ghost

He is torn apart easily.

A convoy of mourning led by a hearse,

Hums along Albert Road like a curse,

Death visited, not for the first, not for the last,

A mother to a son carried away into the past,

Wreaths etch out the words

Written by her grieving family,

Like a paper ghost

She has gone to a place they will one day see.

Heads of people they pass bow in respect,

It is a period of time for them to reflect

On their mortality, the brief chasm of their lives,

Eyes fixated on the funeral cortège,

A ritual, a cycle, continuing forever an age,

They mourn for a moment for this mother

Lying in peace in her terminal sanctuary,

Like a paper ghost

She has gone to a place they will one day see.

Like paper ghosts

They have gone to a place we will one day see,

Like paper ghosts

They are torn apart easily,

Like paper ghosts

Their hollow eyes stare endlessly,

Like paper ghosts

They were never meant to be,

Like paper ghosts

They cling onto dying trees,

Like paper ghosts

They drown in treacherous seas,

Like paper ghosts

They drift on the autumn breeze,

Like paper ghosts

They just want to be free.

You

Where are you,

My solitary cigarette,

Caught in the pavement cracks,

Isolated thoughts passing

Across gulfs between the shadows.

Where are you,

My ray of light glowing,

Piercing darkened clouds,

Specks of your essence

Replacing my doubts.

Stay with me,

My xylophone chiming

For me a tune of our love,

Even if it's only temporary,

Let us not dwell on trivialities,

Just savour the moment,

My melancholy is redundant.

Where are you,
My distant pulsing beacon,
Guiding me to your person,
I follow with moistened eyes
And all the times we said goodbye
Heavy in my heart.

I almost lost you,
Like a dove deceased,
Delicately crushed and bleeding on cobbles
That crease the concrete of my thoughts,
Paranoia lapping because we quarrelled,
I fear our love will become another fossil.

I will find you,
My solitary obsession,
In the crevasses of my dreams,

Within dimensions never seen
Or conceived by mortal men,
It dwells within you too.

When I have you,
The waking world flutters away,
Those concepts of death
Whither and cease to be,
All of my insecurities, fleeing,
Issues no longer inordinate,
My love for you, incumbent.

You call to me,
I reach through murky waters,
All preconceived notions of life
Swim into your arms,
I slip away, dissolving,
Gaining clarity as I hear your voice,
A lullaby fading into the dead of night.

If there ever was a choice,

It would be you.

Always you.

Only you.

You.

The End

Well, don't mind me,
And don't mind them,
For you my friend,
It has all come to an end.

Printed in Great Britain
by Amazon

25766538R00111